I love it!

Written and illustrated by
Shoo Rayner

Collins

Brook is afraid of lots of things.
He is afraid of hunting, fishing and
getting wet.

He is afraid of flight, too.
"I will help you, Brook," Dad tells him.

Dad hunts in the green lagoon.

"The green lagoon is soaking wet!"
Brook complains.

"Come on, Brook! You might like it!"
Dad tells him.

"I do not like the green lagoon,"
Brook claims. "I love it!"

Dad scoops up a shrimp.

"Yuck! Shrimps!" Brook groans.
"Come on! You might like them!"
Dad tells Brook.

Brook scoops up a shrimp from the soft, brown mud.

Scoop!

"I do not like shrimps," Brook snorts.
"I love them!"

9

Dad and Brook creep up a steep cliff.

Dad flaps off. Brook looks down.

Brook shivers in fright.
"I am afraid!" he wails.
"Come on! You might like it!"
Dad tells Brook.

Brook flaps. Then he swoops and floats on the wind.

"Dad," hoots Brook. "I do not like flight ... I love it!"

Brook's flight

After reading

Letters and Sounds: Phase 4

Word count: 170

Focus on adjacent consonants with long vowel phonemes, e.g. *green*

Common exception words: of, he, I, you, the, love, come, like, do

Curriculum links: Science: Animals including humans

National Curriculum learning objectives: Reading/word reading: apply phonic knowledge and skills as the route to decode words; read accurately by blending sounds in unfamiliar words containing GPCs that have been taught; Reading/comprehension: understand both the books they can already read accurately and fluently and those they listen to by making inferences on the basis of what is being said and done

Developing fluency

- Read the book together with your child, using different voices for Dad and Brook.
- You could read Dad's spoken words and your child could read Brook's. You could read the narrator's words together.

Phonic practice

- Encourage your child to practise reading words that contain two or three syllables.
  - Point to **hunting** on page 2. Ask your child to sound out and blend each chunk or syllable (h/u/n/t – i/ng)
  - Repeat for: page 3 **afraid** (a – f/r/ai/d); page 4 **lagoon** (l/a – g/oo/n); page 11 **shivers** (sh/i/v – er/s)

Extending vocabulary

- Look at pages 4–5. Ask your child the following, focusing on specific words:
  - What words could we use instead of **hunts**? (e.g. *searches for, looks for*)
  - On page 4, Brook is complaining. What tone of voice would you use if you were complaining? (*moaning, groaning*)
  - On page 5, what other encouraging word or phrase could you use instead of **Come on**? (e.g. *Do it; Go for it; Try it*)

Comprehension

- Turn to pages 14–15 and ask your child to retell the story in their own words using the pictures linked with arrows as prompts.